for Colin

Text copyright © Michaela Morgan 1988
Illustrations copyright © Sue Porter 1988
All rights reserved.

First published in the U.S.A. 1988
by E. P. Dutton,
2 Park Avenue, New York, N.Y. 10016,
a division of NAL Penguin Inc.

Produced by Mathew Price Ltd

Printed in Hong Kong
First American Edition   OBE
ISBN: 0-525-44371-1   LC: 87-71773
10 9 8 7 6 5 4 3 2 1

Edward Hurts His Knee

written by Michaela Morgan
illustrated by Sue Porter

E. P. Dutton   New York

Edward and his mother were going to visit Grandma.
Edward was very excited. He ran...

and skipped...

and hopped...

and fell. SPLAT!

Edward told his grandma all about his accident.
She thought he had been very brave.